TWENTY-FOUR-H(

CW00351550

CABINET BOOKS, NEW YORK

Inspired by literary precedents such as automatic writing, by the resourcefulness of the *bricoleur* making do with what is at hand, and by the openness toward chance that all artistic production under severe constraint must necessarily incorporate, Cabinet's "24-Hour Book" series invites a number of distinguished authors and artists to be incarcerated in its gallery space to complete a project from start to finish within twenty-four hours.

This volume and its companion — Jeff Dolven's *Take Care* — are the result of an unusual experiment. They were written in the exact same twenty-four-hour period, with O'Reilly working in a room at the Inner Temple in London and Dolven installed at Cabinet's gallery space. Both writers were asked to respond to a prompt, which was revealed to them one day in advance. The prompt took the form of a found document — the 1986 catalogue for Braintree Scientific, an American company that manufactures lab products used in experiments on rats and mice. A pdf of the catalogue is available at <cabinetmagazine. org/books/24Hours_Dolven_Oreilly.php>. Readers may wish to consult it before reading this book.

Written between 12:00 pm British Summer
Time, 19 May 2017 and 12:00 pm British
Summer Time, 20 May 2017

The Ambivalents

Sally O'Reilly

No. 6 in Cabinet's "24-Hour Book" series

Sally O'Reilly writes for performance, page, and video, interleaving academic research and technical knowledges with the comic, the fantastical, and the psycho-social.

Besides contributing to several art magazines and numerous exhibition catalogues, she has written the novel *Crude* (Eros Press, 2016), the libretto for the opera *The Virtues of Things* (Royal Opera, Aldeburgh Music, Opera North, 2015), a monograph on Mark Wallinger (Tate Publishing, 2015), and *The Body in Contemporary Art* (Thames & Hudson, 2009).

She was writer-in-residence at the Whitechapel Art Gallery (2010–2011) and at Modern Art Oxford (2016); producer and co-writer of *The Last of the Red Wine*, a radio sitcom set in the art world (ICA, London, 2011); and co-editor of *Implicasphere* (2003–2008), an inter-disciplinary broadsheet.

Sally O'Reilly in her pyjamas in the Chaucer Room,
Dr Johnson's Buildings, Inner Temple, London,
writing *The Ambivalents*. Photo taken at 4:36 PM
British Summer Time on Friday, 19 May 2017.

To Whom It May Concern:

I am writing to inform you of a fault in one of your products. I recently bought a batch of your DecapiCones™ (product code DC-200) and discovered, eventually, that the opening in the tapered end was missing. As a result, my rats were somewhat compromised in their performance. I have since started making my own openings with a ballpoint pen and will continue to use the rest of the box thus adulterated, but I would appreciate it if you could attend to this so that future dispatches are up to the standard that I have come to expect.

I would also appreciate it if you could provide me with the equivalent in (fully functional) DecapiCones™ as recompense for the rats that were lost to asphyxiation. While I realized the problem before I got through too many, an extra cost was nonetheless incurred in bringing this particular experiment to completion, and so I attach an invoice to cover this.

Yours Sincerely,
Russell Steadman

Dear Jessica,

Thank you for coming and showing us your film. I quite enjoyed it, even if animal testing isn't quite my scene! I hope you enjoyed your visit down here.

I had great fun in the holidays, because I went swimming with my friend Alison on Saturday morning, then in the evening I went to a disco. On Monday and Friday I went to two more discos. On Saturday I took Helen to an IBM disco and we met Alison, Debbie Weir and Emma there. That made four discos in one week! I hope you had as much fun as I did during your time off.

We hope to see you again soon.

Yours sincerely,
Saiful Islam

Dear Mass Bundle

Thank you for coming to visit our school and telling us what you do I really liked the rats I have made you some tasty berries out of rat's eyes

Yours sincerely
Catherine Ellis

To Whom It May Concern:

A family member recently left a copy of your 1986 catalogue at our house following a birthday celebration. The celebration is not really relevant to why I am writing, but I thought I would set a scene for you. People usually send such dull business letters, and I believe that letting people know other sides of our characters makes for better business relationships. The party was excellent, thank you. We had a wheeled trolley loaded up with jellies and junket; we danced the Beguine and the Infernal Gallop. Carriages were at dawn, and drink was taken.

I think from this you can gather the sort of family that we are. And now that the scene is set, I can tell you that I am writing to congratulate you on the cover of your catalogue, and to ask if there are any prior to this one. The member of my family who left this behind did not mention whether you are a new company or not, but as I imagine you would be famous for these covers if you had been around for any amount of time, I can only guess that you are a fledgling company, with bright ideas and an as-yet unjaded attitude.

I love how instead of, in the original, Venus's golden hair lying euphemistically over her — well, over her mound of Venus — in your version it is the rubbery pink tail that stands in for the seat of love of the goddess of same. And I am enjoying the extra tilt of the head for a steeper inclination towards self-deprecation. A humble rat born of the sea, that virgin mother of all creatures? Or a coy rat, a princess even, of mysterious depths?

As well as admiring your work, I was also wondering if you would be interested in me designing future covers for your catalogues. I am not an artist myself, and so could not actually make the covers. That is to say, I could not paint or draw them, but I could design them in words for someone else to execute. While I have not designed book covers before, I have bought many books, and know very well what is eye-catching. My feeling is that your iconoclastic cover is a good start, but there are many other possible ideas that you have so far overlooked. Here are some to whet your appetite:

Idea One: A portrait of a rat in the period style of Henry VIII, grasping not a staff but a test tube of red liquid issuing improbably round and hard-looking effervescent bubbles. The tunic would be decorated not with inert ornamental patterning, but with symbols—moons, ankhs, Mars, and Venus symbols—to connote non-specific but serious knowledge. And the rat could stare at us down his snout, at the bottom of which two long teeth could make a mockery of his patriarchal gravitas.

Idea Two: The coffinette of Tutankhamun's viscera, but with a real furry rat's face. The background would be decorated with diagrammatic representations of scarab beetles, and scissors would make a great faux-hieroglyphic motif.

Idea Three: A dynamic scene in which rats of the world are competing in the 400-meter sprint. The manly chest of the USA rat is about to burst through the winning tape, of course!

Idea Four: A rat wearing a white coat (the pockets filled with syringes, scissors, and other household objects that imply science) sitting at a visual display unit. Onscreen, we see the cursor pointing at a rat or a mouse about to enter a maze—the implication being that the operative rat is showing the onscreen rodent the way. The rat controls the position of the cursor using a tiny geek (also in a white coat, with a cable coming out the top of his head) on a mouse mat that looks like Gruyere.

I have many more ideas where these came from, but I think that, in essence, a global and multi-epochal outlook, with a nod to the arts, would really position your company brilliantly in what I am sure is a competitive market.

I look forward to hearing from you.

Mark Jones

Dear Ms. Brindle,

You may recall that we met on the train a couple of weeks ago. I hope that you don't mind me writing to you at work. I happened to remember the name of your company because I have a dear old friend who grew up in Braintree, and so it was not difficult to track you down in your lair, as I picture all offices. Being a freelancer and always on impersonal, rattling trains, I think of those of you with stable jobs in temperature-controlled offices, swaddled to your oxters in hay and flapjacks, living out the cold nights and shrill days in familiar comfort. Please do correct me if I am wrong though.

I also hope that you do not think me too 'fast' for getting in touch. It is just that I enjoyed our conversation so much, I thought I would try to continue it in another form. And anyway, I am not especially interested in pleasures of the flesh at all, given that my flesh now hangs in fulsome drapes, so you can put any worries about ulterior motives entirely to one side. Give me a nice cup of tea any day, as the teenagers would say that Boy George would say. Having said that though, I do favour Lapsang Souchong over any other tea, so I suppose I do have preferences of some stripe or other. I do not think that makes me a predatory monster though.

If you remember, the crux of our conversation was the notion of ambivalence. I was very much in favour of it as a progressive state. You weren't entirely sure.

One might say that your jury was out. And you may also remember that the conversation arose on my discovering the nature of your paid work. (As opposed to all those wonderful hobbies that you told me about. I am still trying to picture your soap-carving rendition of Serra's *Tilted Arc*—please do send me a photograph if you can.)

Anyway, if you are so inclined, I would be interested to hear more about your thoughts on whether we can indeed hold opposing ideas in our heads at once, or whether it is a symptom of our paradoxical times. Am I deluding myself that two thoughts co-exist? Am I actually switching swiftly between two frameworks of judgement to suit my fluxing situation? Is my sub-conscious even more of a sycophant than I am?

These are not serious questions that I expect you to answer. But please do tell me what instruments you are currently promoting, so that I may taunt my squeamish side with images of torture, and then torture my logical side with accusations of cold-hearted self-interest. I know that at my age I need all the help I can get to hold this elastic sack of giblets together, and so I salute you and your colleagues, all the while feeling relief and guilt at our collective position at the top of the food pile.

With best wishes,
Bernard Limbrey

Dear Herr Braintree,

I am in the writing to you, for I have the displeasure of in my hand holding the Katalog of your despicable Geräten. I am in the writing to you from beyond the Eisener Vorhang, for which I am pleased that it hangs between me and your Geräten.

In my cultural importations, I have, among other Dingen, an X-ray pressed with the music of your Madonna ('Papa Do Not Preach'), which I am finding ironisieren given your Katalog which my contacts also imported. Ironisieren because I am being given to be believing that the Madonna song sings about the subject of Minderjährige Schwangerschaft. In your decadent West you are singing on the one-handed about your fruchtbarkeit, and with the other handed you scrape Rats.

I am writing not in the hoping of answers, but to be in the letting of your knowing that there are other lebensweisen beside your degraded Welt. I draw the Eisener Vorhang closer shutted behinded me.

With pleasure,
Ruth Hitschmann

Dear Miss Jessica,

Thank you for coming to visit our school and for showing us your film. My teacher told us that it is because of what you do that we are a free society, and that we can live longer than cavemen, although I would like to be a caveman when I grow up, because it looks fun, like camping. But then I would like to turn back into me again so that I can live longer than a caveman and be a policeman too.

It was very interesting to see all your tools. I have a pet rabbit. Can you please send me one of those tools that takes its head off? I also like flying daddy longlegs like kites, but my mum gets cross when I use her sewing thread.

I hope you enjoyed your visit to our school. We had egg curry for lunch after you left.

Yours sincerely,
Catherine Le Quesne

Dear Braintree Scientific,

I have great pleasure in informing you that Braintree Scientific, Inc. has been longlisted for the Humane Instruments Prize.

The judges were particularly impressed by the unique circular blade design in the Braintree Scientific Small Animator Decapitator. Mrs. Victoria Teggin, the chair of the judging panel, has written: "Jam-proof precision cutting is vital for swift, painless dispatch. The industry needs more measures like this to meet the expectations of an increasingly humane humanity."©

If you would like to use this quotation in your marketing material, please note that it has been registered and copyrighted, and is subject to a small duplication fee.

To be considered for the shortlist, there is a small administrative fee payable. Please see the attached invoice, which must be paid in full by June 3rd, 1986 for your company to be progressed to the next round.

Kind regards,
Kellie Lashbrook

Dear Human,

I am writing to register my fathomless horror at your enterprise. Where to begin? At the beginning would be the obvious place, but I will have to build up to that. Let me start with your universal rat restrainer.

Clearly you have no understanding of the complexity of the rat. There is no "universal." We are an idiomatically sensitive species, each with our proclivities and needs to which your pachydermal souls are blind. (You may think that a mixed metaphor, but you do not even know that we rats see with our eyes, whiskers, and skin.) That we all seem the same to you is typical of a race that has pressed great sectors of itself into slavery. Everything to you is black or white, big or small, you or not you.

That you send individuals from your own species into space to die in barbaric rituals of technological hubris and hide your own shit inside pipes underground (I know because I have clambered through great frothing bergs of it) does not surprise me at all. That you design universal rat restrainers so that operatives can, and I quote, "relax" should not jolt me out of my reverie either. And yet I am continually perplexed by your casual sensuousness in the face of the death of those that are not you. You acknowledge that our cousins, the mice, have "delicate skin" and "fine hair," as if you were savoring the delights of spring light and a

18

moderate breeze on a girl's nape. You provide each pair of clippers with a can of "clipperoil," whatever plant that might have been wrung from, presumably so that you can get yet another kick out of the small, mean contradictions you contrive to put us creatures through. And then, finally, when you have shaved and slathered us, you use us as fleshy urns in which to boil up vile pestilences so that you can have pills that make the females of your species infertile and your infants survive so that they may come to understand the horrors that are perpetrated in their name. Perversion everywhere.

I scarcely know where I am headed with this letter, or what I hope to achieve by sending it. I feel that I have as much chance of turning your macabre fascination with our innards into valiant inter-species empathy as sand has of becoming intelligent. Perhaps I can simply point out that the only reason you believe your needs to be more pressing than ours is because you have dragged some stuff out of the ground and pressed and crimped it into weapons that make you feel big. Well, let me tell you this: I have friends in low, dark, damp places, and there are billions of them. The bigger you become, the more room you provide for these hordes in search of a host.

Yours,
Coningsby

Dear Ms. Brindle,

I was delighted to receive your reply. One gets so used to sending huge bellows of camaraderie out into the wide world and getting such meagre ripples in reply. I am also very glad to hear that all is well at that end, and that the conference was so fruitful for you. Congratulations on the longlisting too. May the best animal tester win!

As for your concerns regarding my health, I am afraid that I have rather overplayed my frailty. Apart from a verruca (should there be an 'h' in there some-where?) that I have been harbouring for some twenty years and a bilious response to fructose, I am really rather well.

And in response to your question about ambivalence: yes and no.

I am afraid that I am in rather a hurry today—against the clock as ever—and so must sign off already. I just didn't want you to think that your reply had been left unreplied. I will write a more elucidating response soon, once I have scraped this deadline off my wall planner.

All best wishes,
Bernard Limbrey

Dear Mrs. Jessica Brindle,

I am writing to you as a representative of the beagle community. We, the beagles, are fed up with ignorant, lazy people automatically associating us with smoking. I am writing to you in your capacity as the public relations officer of an organization that would also probably very much like to eradicate this association, not only because it is a cliché, but also because the world has moved on and I no longer know any beagles who smoke. We are, on the whole, more health-conscious these days.

Certainly, clichés become clichés for a reason, but this is not to say that they continue to be relevant. It is for this purpose that we should work together to try and install a new image of beagles in the common consciousness. A new, more accurate cliché, if you like. We, the beagles, feel that a much more accurate and positive representation of our participation in human experimentation would be some nice glossy photographs of your Vascular-Access-Port™, installed subcutaneously and perhaps even with a catheter inserted and in the process of sampling blood or infusing drugs or disease.

My proposal is that together we generate a high-concept photographic campaign, to be distributed as posters and on television, displacing those frankly erroneous pictures of beagles dragging on a cigarette. I am proposing a collaboration, since I can provide the beagles, and you, I am inferring from your excellent catalogue, can provide the photography and distribution, as well as abundant Vascular-Access-Ports™.

We, the beagles, believe this will be in all our interests. Please let us know your thoughts at your earliest convenience.

Yours Faithfully,
Maxwell

The Beagle is a happy-go-lucky breed with a wonderful disposition.

For the attention of the Marketing Department, Braintree Scientific

Let me introduce myself. I am a literary critic known for my vivisection of overwrought prose. If you require a paragraph spatchcocked or clam-shelled, I'm your girl.

I felt I should get in touch because, even though we have certain interrogative tendencies in common, I am compelled to remind you that there is more to animals than mere flesh and sinews. In your dedication to the empirical, it seems to me that you are overlooking the metaphysical and metaphorical qualities of beasts. And as you search for similarities with the human to capitalize on, you miss their motley differences. Poor you.

To refresh your memory of the ungraspable, I have garnered all mentions of animals in a single book written by the bestially indefatigable Updike. Before you read on, I should clarify that none of these animals are actual. Do not reach for your scalpel or guillotine or buzz saw. I hope that this is not too confusing.

With best wishes,
Ayesha Hasan

Brown legs probably, bitty birdy breasts. Their skin under the fur gets all loose like a puppy's neck. The animal in him swells its protest that he is going west. The road twists more and more wildly in its struggle to

23

gain height and then without warning sheds its skin of asphalt and worms on in dirt. They are monkeys, Harry. Women are monkeys. It was like the hides of a thousand lizards stitched together. Each hair passing in the light through a series of tints, like the hair of a dog. You were a young deer, he continues, with big feet. Where her foreshortened calves hang like tan fish. About five two and ugly as a monkey. You know, you're a pig really. The muscles and lips and bones of her expanded underside press against him as a new anatomy of another animal. A tin-smelling coldness he associates with the metal that makes up the walls of a cave and the ribs of its floor, delicate rhinoceros grey, mottled with the same disease linoleum has. As a shark nudges silent creases of water ahead of it, the green fender makes ripples of air that break against the back of Rabbit's knees. On the concrete-and-plank benches fluffy old men like pigeons, dressed in patches of grey multiple as feathers. My queen, he says, my good horse. She asks, Are you really a rat? Eccles, looking like a young owl, awkward, cross, pops out of the kitchen. As he and Eccles walk together toward the first tee he feels partially destroyed, like a good horse yoked to a pulpy-hoofed nag. Words hang like caterpillar nests that can't be brushed away. Awkwardness spiders at his elbows. Harry loved those salmon colors so. She was drunk as a monkey anyway. Those little snips running around her at hockey in gym like a cow in that blue uniform like a baby suit. Your husband's running around a few miles away with some bat. The kitten's instinct to kill the spool with its cotton paws. In worming against her warmth he has pulled her dress up from her knees. She's heavy in bed and once in a while looks at him as if he's some sort of pig. She has a pigeon-toed way of sauntering. It is as if electricity, that amazingly trained mouse, has scurried through miles of wire only to gnaw at the end of its errand on an impenetrable plate of metal. His white shirt seems to crawl, like a cluster of glow worms in grass. She lies there like some dead animal. The shaved planes above his ear shine like the blue throat feathers of a pigeon. If you're sitting there like a buzzard young man hoping she's going to die. He draws backward into sleep like a turtle drawing into its shell. While the claws of a bear rattle like rain outside. His own actions slid from him, oil off a duck. He is concentrating on her skin, trying to see if it does look like a lot of little lizard skins sewn together. Like the body of a bird. Colors that no-one could live with, salmon and aqua and a violet like the violet that kills germs on toilet seats in gas stations. He shall feed his flock like a shepherd: he shall gather the lambs with his arms, and carry them in his bosom. Clogged with spider-fine twigs. A darkness in defiance of the broad daylight whose sky leaps in jagged patches from treetop to treetop above him like a silent monkey. In the treacherous light the slope of land is like some fleeing, twisting creature. Up in the sea of sky a lake of

25

fragmented mackerel clouds drifts in one piece like a
school of fish. Her voice had gotten up on a hard little
high horse. You're not a rat, you don't stink, you're not
enough to stink.

Dear Jessica Bundle,

My name is Annmarie, my friends call me Bumpy. I liked your film when you came to our school. Miss told us that you are clever and I will not be clever. I like mice. And I prefer lamb.

Yours truly truly,
Annmarie Harris

Dear Jessica (if I may be so bold),

Thank you for the photograph of the *Tilted Arc*. It really is a feat of soft engineering. I am agog at your evident patience. The humility of the substance brings real charge to the form too. Enough of those silly men flinging lead and steel about. This is real sensitive craft.

And I am sorry for leaving you dangling as to my answer to your initial question. Yes, I do feel that the capacity for ambivalence is somehow pegged to age, but I also believe that it is at work constantly, from the moment we struggle out into this cold, complicated world. I have felt that Eros and Thanatos have been locked together in a battle for my soul from the get-go, but I am only now coming to know to describe it thus. This is why I can look at your photographs of cleaved mice and bald monkeys and feel both horror and relief: horror that I must feel a dull ache of the object lost forever; relief that the object will itself retreat from me eventually, and I from it. Perhaps the young can be ambivalent because they have yet to widen the focus of their care. Their emotional entanglements are few and simple. The old can be ambivalent because too large an inventory of care has passed through our knobbled fingers. We have loved and lost so much that we are numbed from the scarring.

This is only my own foolish old perspective on the matter, of course. There is, I am told, a scale by which ambiguity tolerance can be measured. The insane are very tolerant, I hear, and artists also claim to be (although I suspect that this is a pose). But ambiguity is an external state that can be accepted or rejected. Ambivalence, on the other hand, is an internal state to be inhabited. I am not sure that there can be a degree of tolerance or otherwise for ambivalence. One simply finds oneself made up out of it.

Did you now that the Stoics believed speech to be battered air, shaped by the tongue to carry meaning? Knowledge, stored in the body, would receive this battered air. If all went well, if the battered air was of sound rationale, the soul would remain healthy and the body of knowledge would continue to grow. But if the battered air contained an ambiguity, the body of knowledge could be infected by a misunderstanding and the soul corrupted. Ambiguity intolerance is once thing, but what I want to know is whether the Stoics were able to feel ambivalent about anything. What would that mean to the body of knowledge? Would it then flicker between solidity and wind?

As you can probably tell, I do like a mechanical model, where I can account for all the moving parts. All this computing nonsense is not for me. Those boxes and invisible powers make me shudder. Please do tell me more about this new thermal pad of yours though. I wonder—do you make them large enough for tired old men with rusted joints?

All best wishes to you and yours,
Bernard Limbrey

heinous intrAvenous the Rapists

Dear Ms. Jessica Brindle,

Regarding our conversation last Tuesday, I am hereby sending you the requisite information, as requested.

Payments are not made piecemeal on the receipt of information. Rather, you would enter the employ of the police force as a salaried officer. You would be free to continue in your current position, although this would, of course, present certain difficulties. We generally counsel the adoption of what we term an "illusory position," the details of which you are familiar with or which you can research, but which does not present any palpable contradiction with the new role assigned to you.

I have enclosed a handbook called *The Presentation of the Illusory Self in Everyday Life* for your consultation. It outlines certain lines that should not be crossed, but we recognize that you cannot be held accountable for the actions of those to whom you present your illusory self. It should also be noted that, while the force takes every step to protect your real identity, it will not perjure itself in the event of exposure, prosecution, or paternity/maternity.

Sincerely,
Officer Hallon

Dear Jessica,

Thank you for showing us the film of your pets. It was very nice and you have a lot of fun. I have written you a song and made you a painting.

I love you Pegasus
But you've been mendacious
Naughty little mouse
In alcohol I'll you douse

See how Pegasus
Is hilarious
Lumpy little thing
This is going to sting

My darling Pegasus
Held up in a truss
Your skin like taffeta
Pierced by a catheter

God bless Pegasus
No more salaciousness
I have your ovaries
and other pink sund-a-ries

Yours sincerely,
Suki Johal

St. Kilda House Mouse.

Dear Braintree Scientific,

Please let me introduce myself. I am a writer based in G–. I have been writing professionally for eighteen years, and have published several books and written two plays, which have been performed in venues around Europe. I have enclosed my cv so that you can get a better idea of what I have done to date.

I am writing because I would like to offer myself as a writer-in-residence at your company. I am currently looking for a context for my upcoming project, and thought that Braintree Scientific could be the perfect place.

I have been noticing for some time now that the scientific and the emotional are somewhat detached from one another. It is as if the "two cultures war," if you recall that skirmish of so many years ago now, has been rumbling on and on, like a feud that becomes part of a family's identity. I believe we have simply normalized the separation between the technical and the expressive, and never again shall the twain... Certainly, people talk of expressing themselves by taking Polaroids, or they take a train to go to a wedding, where they'll have a jolly good cry. But no one really thinks of the camera or the train as being anything other than the cold, hard apparatus by which these warmer, softer matters are served up.

It is my contention that technology has got a bad rap. I would like to redress the assumption that science is populated by hard-nosed, hard-hearted automata who simply push buttons and then read the telemetry that comes out (or up?). I would like to come to Braintree Scientific and write an opera—that most humanizing of forms—about what goes on in your industry, and in your very own offices and warehouses in particular.

You might think it strange that I would want to write an opera about a laboratory supplies company and not about the laboratories that you supply. My answer to that is aesthetic: the animal-testing lab would be too obvious a source of drama. I am interested in the reality of science and technology, the everyday grind. Dissection and testing would be too vivid to actually show—there would be a mess of ribbons and lasers everywhere—but its resonance there in the background of what you do would indeed lend an operatic timbre!

Previous experience tells me that I should emphasize that although I work in the arts, I am not necessarily against animal testing. I am genuinely interested in the subject, since lab animals lie tethered at the intersection between emotional attachment and scientific objectivity. My apparently liberal politics can put people's back up. When I was younger, working as a temp, I was sent home from a chicken factory at lunchtime because someone found out that I was a vegetarian. They assumed I was a saboteur and marched me off the premises without pay. But, I can assure you that I would only be interested in representing your work in a positive light, as valuable to a fully rounded society that is mature enough to love Spot or Rufus, while eating venison and growing old thanks to all those pharmaceuticals.

I would be very happy to talk through my ideas with you in more detail, should you be interested in hosting me as a writer-in-residence. I look forward to hearing from you.

All best wishes,
Emily Beer

Dear Jessica,

Thank you for the Deltaphase™ Isothermal Pad. I am thrilled with it. I use it to keep my cod livers just above chambré. Things slip down much easier when they are closer to one's own body temperature. Oh dear, that does sound unfortunately crude, but I can assure you it is all above board. The English language has been booby-trapped, has it not?

And thank you also for your thoughtful response to my rather garbled drivellings about ambivalence. I need to get the rubble out the way first, before I can get to the gold, but I do wish I would keep such excavations within the privacy of my own head. You, on the other hand, are a wise woman beyond your ears.

That is a very good question you pose about ambivalence and animals. Perhaps it is, as you suggest, a luxury state only afforded us 'higher' mammals. The base instincts of dogs do always seem clear-cut, it is true, but may I venture that they are baser in relation to some things more than others. My beagle is distinctly uninterested in fish, but will force some down if there's nothing else. I'm not sure that's strictly ambivalence. I'm not suggesting that she doesn't like the taste but knows that fish is good for her. It's more to propose that equivocalness is not the prerogative of humans alone. Although, you are right when you point out how mixed or vague feelings can be frightfully useful in social situations. If fluidity is at the root of care—the ability to make shapes around others—then ambivalence is definitely a mechanism for adaptability and all for the good.

As ever, I am being over-physical in my analogies. I am an old Stoic at heart. But it does not mean that I don't reserve a little appreciation for the alchemical too. The *je ne sais quoi* of your recent soap carving brought a lump to my throat. Bravo!

I am sending you a packet of tea—some Lapsang Souchong. I hope it refreshes the parts!

All best,
Bernard Limbrey

Dear Sir or Madam,

I am a researcher working in the UK. A colleague from abroad recently gave me a copy of your excellent catalogue, which I read cover to cover. I was heartened to see how wide a range of products you carry, and how rigorous your understanding of the industry I work in is.

Here in the UK we have our own suppliers. They are fine, but they do not offer, for instance, the Deltaphase™ Isothermal Pad. Instead, we repurpose old railway foot warmers containing acetate solution, which is at least one rung up the technological ladder from hot water. And instead of gloves made out of the same material as anti-shark suits, we must make do with rubber gloves and regular tetanus jabs.

Reading your catalogue gave me an insight into the practice of my discipline beyond this parochial island. I have glimpsed a vista of bulk ordering, cutting-edge kit, and a scale of operation that is truly inspiring. Also, to work with baboons and horses (as mentioned in your excellent Vascular-Access-Port write-up) instead of mice is now my new ambition—something I could not have dreamed possible before I read your catalogue.

And so I come to the reason for my writing to you like this. It is very difficult here in the UK to contact fellow practitioners. They are all ex-directory on account of the numerous anti-vivisection leagues that the universities seem to specialise in grooming these days.

Also, I suspect that these other companies are subject to the same limitations of scale and species as my own laboratories. Everything in this country is, notoriously, smaller and meaner. I would really appreciate it if you could send me a list of companies that you supply so that I can send them my curriculum vitae. Now that I have seen how things are run elsewhere, I am ready to take the plunge into a whole new continent!

Thank you in advance for your help.

Yours Truly,
Anushka Kangesu

Urgent (by hand)
To the woman in the beige raincoat and red shoes who
works at Braintree Scientific

I saw you from the bus yesterday, Crumpet Blonde. I
could make you happy. I'm the most dissolute woman of
them all. I'm abusing myself in loneliness with my fingers. No one sees my classy underwear. I want to show
them to someone. I love muff-diving and I do a good
blowjob. I have big nipples and a slim body. I demand
nothing. I have a friend — she is 19 years old. If you
want to see us playing with each other then come to us.
Wet student girls do many awesome things in bed. You
haven't seen asses like this before — like globes — everything is natural. I am ready to let you touch it and fuck
me, to lick you through and swallow up every drop.

I have huge soft boobies, the softest bum, long legs
and no principles, and I wear only expensive clothes. I'm
23 years old, with ginger hair and slim fit. I smell like
orchid and sin. I'm a juicy sweet young fairy. Cinnamon
and sin are the scent of me. Love's been licked and when
someone makes me obey, my holes are ready to take you
in. Quick start! Long action! Are you free today?

All Yours,
Angel

Dear Jessica,

In answer to your query, dated 05/03/86, there have been no known cases of polymer atrophy in Micro-Renathane® Implantation Tubing, and the substance maintains its status as 'medical grade' according to your own criteria. While, as you point out, there is no universal grading system that defines the parameters of this designation, you have, as manufacturers, had significant experience of the material and have never, according to records, received up-stream feedback to the contrary. I believe that I am confident in saying that you may consider it safe for all internal uses.

I would be happy to meet when I am next in Massachusetts if you are developing a new product that requires reviewing. As you mention, blood compatibility would lend itself to several internal applications, although I am not sure what you mean by its 'shapeliness.' Having said that, the attached graph does seem to speak to your hypothesis. The required probability here also falls within arbitrarily calibrated medical safety thresholds of gradient and surface area, as designated by the industry itself.

All best wishes,
Anthony Allston

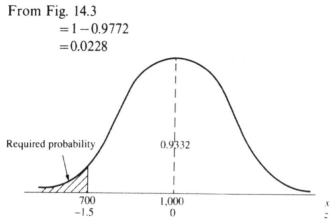

From Fig. 14.3
$$= 1 - 0.9772$$
$$= 0.0228$$

Required probability

0.9332

700
−1.5

1,000
0

x

z

Fig. 14.1

Dearest Jessica,

I can only apologise for my tardy response. My time has not been my own. Although having said that, I don't know quite whose it has been. Perhaps I have simply been dallying. Probably because I must confess that I have fibbed to you a tad. I have something a little graver than a verruca (at last, I have learned that there is no 'h'). Soon I will be entirely bald, as they say in Spain. Despite medicine's best efforts, I am not likely to be writing many more letters. I am clutching my Deltaphase™ Isothermal Pad, and I feel quite calm about things. Interestingly, I note that I am perfectly passionate about my ambivalence towards the end. The paradoxes persist, even at this stage.

I wish you well, and hope that those anti-vivisectionists cut you some slack, as they no doubt say. I reckon I have eked a few extra months as a result of your industry, but I shall soon depart for the Bruegel-like realm where the rats and monkeys get to invent the instruments. Wish me luck.

Yours,
Bernard Limbrey

Dear Mrs. Jessica Brindle,

I am writing to you as a representative of the ape and monkey community. We, the apes and monkeys, are fed up with ignorant, lazy people automatically associating us with tea parties. I am writing to you in your capacity as the public relations officer of an organization that would also probably very much like to eradicate this association, not only because it is a cliché, but also because the world has moved on and I no longer know any primates who attend parties. We are, on the whole, more health-conscious these days.

Certainly, clichés become clichés for a reason, but this is not to say that they continue to be relevant. It is for this purpose that we should work together to try and install a new image of apes and monkeys in the common consciousness. A new, more accurate cliché, if you like. We, the apes and monkeys, feel that a much more accurate and positive representation of our participation in human experimentation would be some nice glossy photographs of your Vascular-Access-Port™, installed subcutaneously and perhaps even with a catheter inserted and in the process of sampling blood or infusing drugs or disease.

My proposal is that together we generate a high-concept photographic campaign, to be distributed as posters and on television, displacing those frankly erroneous pictures of apes and monkeys sipping tea. I am proposing a collaboration, since I can provide the apes and monkeys, and you, I am inferring from your excellent catalogue, can provide the photography and distribution, as well as abundant Vascular-Access-Ports™.

We, the apes and monkeys, believe this will be in all our interests. Please let us know your thoughts at your earliest convenience.

Yours Faithfully,
Perks

Dear Sir or Madam,

I am an art student, about to complete my masters in Fine Art at CalArts. I would like to ask you to sponsor my upcoming degree show. I do not require cash, but sponsorship in kind, in the form of three Multi-Speed Syringe Pumps. I am planning to inject the food of three flamingos with blue food coloring at a rate of change dictated by Saint Saëns's "Bacchanal" from *Samson and Delilah*, which I have stretched to last the length of the exhibition.

The piece is about humans and nature, the speed of looking and the speed of metabolism, both of which are both human and natural. It is also a disco for birds and an homage to Prince. And it is about freedom and power.

If you like this idea, please send me some pumps at the address above.

Kind Regards,
Simon Birks

Dear Sirs,

I have taken it upon myself to point out to you that while your work in furthering animal science is admirable, it would be far more useful to society if you were to focus more on humans. It is all very well providing equipment that produces knowledge of the endocrine system of a guinea pig and drug metabolism in mice, but there are people dying out here.

Yours Truly,
Adrian Davies

FOOD AND DRINK CONSUMED

Friday, 19 May 2017

> *12:00 PM water (ongoing throughout)*
> *13:55 PM salad of lentils cooked with onions and bay leaves, new potatoes, tomato, pea shoots, capers, olive oil, lemon juice, salt, pepper*
> *14:50 PM two squares of salty chocolate*
> *16:12 PM coffee*
> *19:52 PM pasta with tomato, chilli, coriander and pistachio; baby aubergines stuffed with feta and pine nuts*
> *22:32 PM two squares of salty chocolate*

Saturday, 20 May 2017

> *00:26 AM one aspirin*
> *01:21 AM one piece of bread and butter*
> *4:02 AM seven brazil nuts and six prunes*
> *6:22 AM coffee*
> *7:19 AM one piece of bread and butter*
> *8:47 AM five brazil nuts and four prunes*
> *9:51 AM one banana*
> *10:15 AM lemonade*

The Ambivalents
Sally O'Reilly

Design: Everything Studio
Editor: Sina Najafi

The author would like to thank Richard Salter QC, Bencher of the Honourable Society of the Inner Temple, for organizing her ensconcement in the Chaucer Room, and Henrietta Amodio and Lorna Pay for arranging the finer details. Thanks also to Roxy Beaujolais for bringing a hot dinner from the Seven Stars public house, to Roy Voss for his portrait photography, and to Matt Rogers for ongoing support and the stopping of essential gaps.

Cabinet Books wishes to thank the Andy Warhol Foundation for the Visual Arts for its support of this project.

ISBN: 978-1-932698-80-0
Printed by Bookmobile, Minneapolis, USA.

Published by Cabinet Books
Immaterial Incorporated
181 Wyckoff Street
Brooklyn, NY 11217 USA